IT'S THE GREAT PUMPKIN,
CHARLIE BROWN

It's The Great Pumpkin, Charlie Brown

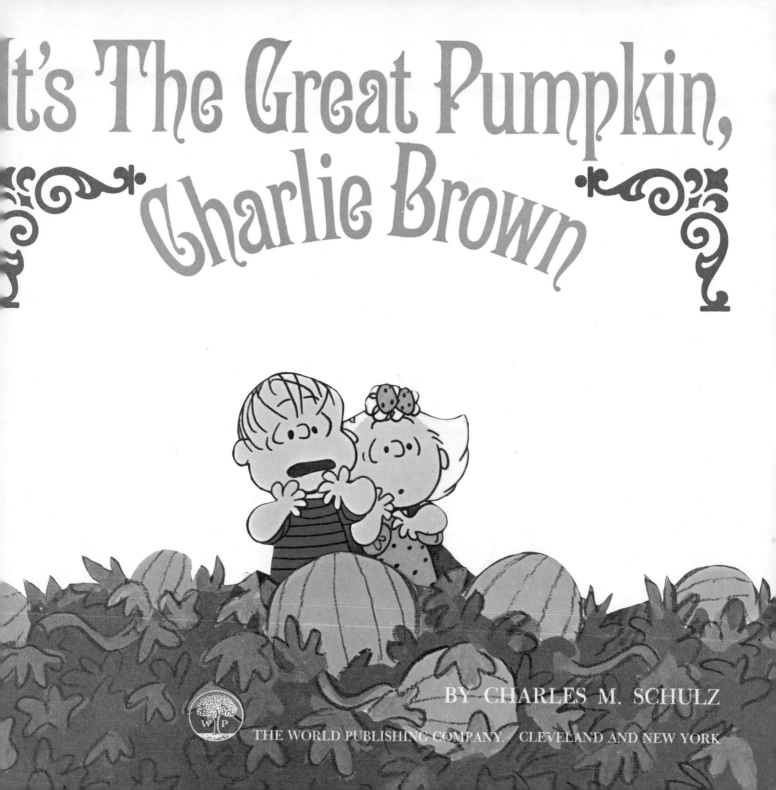

BY CHARLES M. SCHULZ

THE WORLD PUBLISHING COMPANY.   CLEVELAND AND NEW YORK

Published by The World Publishing Company
2231 West 110th Street, Cleveland, Ohio 44102
Published simultaneously in Canada
by Nelson, Foster & Scott Ltd.

First Edition
Copyright © 1967 by United Features Syndicate, Inc.
Produced in association with
Lee Mendelson—Bill Melendez TV Production

Illustrations from the Bill Melendez—Lee Mendelson
television production, "It's the Great Pumpkin,
Charlie Brown!"

DEDICATED TO THE GREAT PUMPKIN

There was a general feeling around the neighborhood that Linus always acted a bit peculiar during the month of October. Each year he got out a piece of his nicest stationery and wrote a letter to someone he called "the Great Pumpkin."

It really annoyed Lucy, his sister, because she thought it made her look bad. Snoopy thought it was the funniest thing he had ever heard.

The only person who thought Linus just might be right about the Great Pumpkin was Sally. She listened very carefully as Linus explained the whole story to her.

"Each year on Halloween night, the Great Pumpkin rises out of the pumpkin patch that he thinks is the most sincere and flies through the air with his pack of toys for all the good little children in the world."

The other kids on the block were much more interested in making costumes to wear when they went out that night for Tricks or Treats. Charlie Brown had intended to look like a ghost, but he had a little trouble with the scissors and ended up looking more like a peeled potato. Lucy was proud of her witch's mask because she always said that a person should wear a costume that was in direct contrast to her actual personality. The most original costume, if you want to call it that, was worn by Snoopy, for he had found a flyer's helmet and goggles and a beautiful scarf. He looked exactly like a World War I flying ace.

Now, Linus had convinced Sally that going out for Tricks or Treats not only was a waste of time, but was downright wrong, for he maintained that the only way to celebrate Halloween was to sit in a pumpkin patch and wait for the arrival of the Great Pumpkin. He told Sally that a person had to be very sincere in his waiting and never say, "*If* the Great Pumpkin comes," but always, "*When* the Great Pumpkin comes." "One little slip like that," declared Linus, "can cause the Great Pumpkin to pass you by!"

They looked around the field where they were crouched, and Linus declared, "The Great Pumpkin just has to pick this patch because it is very sincere. In fact, there is nothing but sincerity here as far as the eye can see."

Lucy, Charlie Brown, and their friends had just finished knocking at the door of a house asking for Tricks or Treats. Lucy had asked for an extra apple "for my stupid brother who can't come along because he is sitting in the pumpkin patch waiting for the Great Pumpkin." Each looked into the bag he was carrying with him. After the others had said they had found things like cookies, candy, gum, and apples, Charlie Brown said, "All I got was a rock!"

No one noticed that Snoopy was missing. He had gone off by himself and had climbed on top of his doghouse, which he pretended was a World War I flying plane.

"Here's the World War I flying ace taking off in his Sopwith Camel." In his imagination he zoomed through the sky while anti-aircraft shells burst all around him. Just then he spotted the enemy plane he was looking for. It was the Red Baron!

Before Snoopy could turn his plane to the attack, the Red Baron swooped down upon him and riddled his plane with bullets.

Smoke poured from behind, and Snoopy fought desperately to control his plane. With amazing skill, he guided his badly damaged Sopwith Camel to a crash landing, and leaped out before the enemy could find him.

Now he had to make his way back
across no-man's land to the aerodrome.

In the meantime, Linus and Sally were still scanning the skies for the appearance of the Great Pumpkin.

"I hope you haven't been trying to fool me," warned Sally, "and if you try to hold my hand, I'll slug you!"

"Listen!" cried Linus. "I hear something!"

There was a low rustle in the grass around the pumpkin patch.

Suddenly a strange silhouette appeared before their eyes. "It's the Great Pumpkin!" cried Linus. "He is rising out of the pumpkin patch!"

He toppled over backward in a faint.

"I've been robbed!" shrieked Sally. "I waited all night in a pumpkin patch, and all I saw was a stupid beagle!"

She grabbed Linus by the front of his shirt and shook him until his eyes rattled. "I believed in you! I missed Tricks or Treats to sit in this pumpkin patch! You owe me restitution!"

Sally stalked off in anger, and Linus
was left alone.

About four o'clock in the morning, Lucy woke up, and decided to see if Linus had come in yet.

His bed was empty.

She put her coat on and went out to the pumpkin patch. There was Linus, curled up on the ground with his blanket. He was so cold, he was shaking all over.

Lucy led him back home and helped him to get into bed.

The next morning, Charlie Brown and Linus were leaning on a wall, staring into space. Each was thinking about last night.

"I went out for Tricks or Treats, and all I got was a bag of rocks!" moaned Charlie Brown. "Did you ever get to see the Great Pumpkin?"

"Nope," said Linus. "He never showed up."

"Well, don't be too disappointed. I've done some stupid things in my life, too."

"STUPID!" shrieked Linus. "What do you mean, 'stupid'? Just wait until next year. I'll find a pumpkin patch, and I'll sit in that pumpkin patch and it'll be a sincere pumpkin patch, and the Great Pumpkin will come! Just you wait and see! I'll sit in that pumpkin patch, and I'll see the Great Pumpkin. Just wait until next year!"

Charlie Brown sighed.